MW01113946

Missy's Lowcountry Adventure

Marilyn Kelsey

ISBN: 1532999062
ISBN 13: 9781532999062
Library of Congress Control Number: 2016907396

Dedication

This book is dedicated to my
three granddaughters!
Melissa Jade (MJ)
Brianna (Breegirl aka Brigirl)
Brittany (Britt)
And to my "adopted" grandson Evan

Thank you to:
My son Bill Kelsey for his
technical skill and assist!

My two daughters:
Beth(the Bluebird) and Maureen(Moey)

Debbie Maltrotti in Millsboro DE

Mary Ogden Fersner in Charleston SC

A special thank you to my husband Bob
for all his encouragement and support!

Contents

Chapter 1
Lost!

The kitten turned around in circles. "OH NO! Where am I? How do I get back home?"

Earlier that morning, Missy, a gray-and-white kitten, opened her eyes as the sun streamed through the window. Squinting from the light, she stretched and glanced over at MJ, who was sleeping beside her. Missy snuggled closer to the little girl for warmth. The kitten loved to cuddle with her new family.

Missy arrived at the Richard's home in Charleston, South Carolina, two weeks ago. The kitten was already spoiled and loved by everyone in the family, especially eight-year-old MJ.

Life was good. She spotted a Carolina bluebird perched outside the window. "What is that?" Missy wondered. She jumped off the bed onto the windowsill to examine the pretty creature. Missy reached for it and tumbled out the window, into a potted palm, and then onto the lawn. She chased the bluebird throughout the neighborhood and down to the park. Then she stopped, looked around, and thought, "Where is that flying thing?"

Then the kitten realized she did not know where she was or how to get home.

Chapter 2
Jet

Missy started to walk and hoped she was going in the right direction. She came upon a group of stores. There was a Little Cricket convenience store, a pizza shop, and a deli. The aroma from the deli made her hungry. She smelled tuna! Yum!

The kitten skirted around to the back of the deli in hopes that she would find some scraps of food.

She came upon several garbage cans. One of them was turned on its side. What luck! The kitten slowly approached the overturned can and peeked in. Something in the back of the can was moving. Missy jumped back, and out from the can appeared a scruffy, rust-colored dog, licking his paws. "Hey," the dog barked. "BEAT IT! This is my can!"

"Sorry. I was hungry and smelled something yummy to eat. I'm lost and cannot find my way home," the kitten said.

The dog instantly felt bad that he had yelled and frightened the kitten. He realized the cat meant no harm. "Okay, I'll share the can with you. Come on in."

Missy pushed her way into the back of the can.

Sure enough, she found the tuna can she wanted and licked every morsel. She was fortunate to also find a half-empty milk carton, and she lapped up the milk until she heard a loud, booming voice shout, "Hey, get out of there!"

"Uh-oh, we need to scoot. Now! That is Mr. Zimmerman. RUN! HIDE!" the dog cried out.

Missy scampered out of the can behind the dog. She glanced back to see the man running after them, waving a broom over his head.

"I'll get you, you bums!" the store owner yelled, swinging the broom at them.

Missy and the dog dashed down the street into a wooded area and then stopped and hid behind a group of palm trees.

"Whew! That was a close call," the dog said. "We should be safe now. You are pretty fast for a kitten. My name is Jet. What's yours?"

"I'm Missy. Thanks for getting me out of there. He looked really mad."

"He doesn't like it when I turn over the garbage cans, but I'm always faster than he is," Jet bragged.

"That was nice of you to share your food with me.

It was so yummy!" Missy said, licking her whiskers. "Where do you live?"

Jet lowered his head. "I don't have a home. My owners were mean to me, so I ran away. I've been on my own for six months now."

"How awful!" Missy said. "Hey, maybe my family can adopt you, like they adopted me. The only thing is, I am lost and can't find my way home."

"Really! That would be so cool! But I'm not too sure about staying with your folks," Jet said. He was not about to trust another family. He had surprised himself by getting chummy with the kitten, but he had been feeling lonely and sort of liked this cheerful, tiny fur ball.

"I have a feeling once you meet my family, you will change your mind. Especially MJ. She is eight years old and hugs me all the time," Missy said.

Even though she had just met Jet, she had a feeling they were going to be friends.

"We'll see," Jet said, not convinced. "Okay, Missy. Are you ready to start our search?"

"Oh yes!"

"Do you know the name of your street?" Jet asked.

"No. I've only lived there a few weeks. But I might remember it if I saw it. And there's a park near my home."

"There are many parks in the area," Jet said.

"Hmm...what should we do first?" the kitten asked.

"We'll check them all out and see if you remember something. Ready?"

"I'm so ready! Thanks for your help, Jet," Missy said.

"Don't thank me yet, little one. Come on! Let's get started."

Chapter 3
How Old Are You?

Jet led Missy to James Island County Park in Charleston. The sun was warm for an October morning, and the area was nearly empty. It was a weekday, and the children were in school.

Missy stared up at the southern pines and large oak trees draped with Spanish moss. "These trees are so big, and the hanging moss looks like giant spider webs," Missy said.

Jet laughed and said, "The Angel Oak trees in South Carolina are over a hundred years old."

"Wow, that's really old. I'm only twelve weeks old. How old are you, Jet?"

"Five, but in dog years, I'm thirty-five."

"You're so smart," Missy said.

Jet blushed. "I read the newspaper every day and watch the Nature Channel whenever I get a chance."

Impressed with his knowledge, Missy was sure that he could lead her home.

Chapter 4
Lather Up...You Stink!

"We're coming to a pond where I like to swim and take a bath. Hurry. I'll race you!" Jet said as he bolted toward the water.

Missy sprinted after him and was thankful he was going to jump into the water. He was really stinky from scrounging around in the garbage cans. She did not want to hurt his feelings by telling him he smelled bad, especially when he was so willing to help her find her family.

Jet dove into the pond, while Missy timidly placed her paws in the water. They heard someone say, "Boy, do you two stink! Peeee U!" They both spun around to see a turtle sunning himself on a big gray rock.

"Back off, bucko!" Jet yelled at the turtle. "We had a bad morning. We were having breakfast, until we were chased by a man with a broom. We barely escaped."

Holding his nose, the turtle said, "Pardon me, Mr. Dog. Didn't mean to snap at you. But you two smell like a garbage dump." He tossed a bar of soap at Jet. "Here's some soap. Lather up!"

Jet worked up the soap into bubbles, splashed around, and swam. The kitten waded playfully by the edge of the pond. Missy preferred to lick her body clean, as cats like to do. She then plopped herself onto her back and rolled around, basking in the sun.

The dog came out of the pond and shook off the water. They both went over to the turtle to introduce themselves.

The turtle said, "Glad to meet you; I'm Frankie. What are you two doing here?"

Jet explained to him that Missy was lost and that he was going to help her find her way home.

"Where do you live, Frankie? Do you have a family?" the kitten asked.

"I have no family," the turtle said, frowning. "I live here in the pond."

"I have a great idea. Why don't you come with Jet and me to my house? We have a big pond in the backyard."

"Do you think your family will like me?" the turtle asked.

"Sure they will." Missy grinned.

"Let's look around the park and see if it looks familiar to you," the turtle said. Missy and Jet tried to walk slower so the turtle could keep up.

Chapter 5
Monkey See, Monkey Do

They came upon a sign that read, "Fun Yard."
"Oh, little one, we have to stop here. It's a play-
ground!" Jet said. "They have swings, a slide, and
monkey bars."

"Monkey bars? What are those?" Missy asked.
"Are there monkeys on them?"

"No, silly. You swing on them like a monkey swinging in the trees."

"How fun!" Missy said, tapping her paws together.
"Do we have time?"

"Sure. It's early. Come on, and I'll push you on the
swings."

For the next half hour, they played, slid down the slide, and climbed the monkey bars.

They made funny faces at each other. Jet did his best impression while hanging upside down. He scratched under his arms with his paws. "Whooooheeee...hahaha!"

Missy and Frankie rolled over on their backs and howled with laughter.

"You are the funniest dog I've ever met!" Frankie said.

Jet gave a bow. "Thank you. Thank you very much. You've been a wonderful audience."

"Jet, boost me up on the bars so I can try," Frankie said. The turtle tried to hang upside down but slipped and fell. Luckily, Jet was there to catch him.

"Frankie, you'd better stick to the ground. You might get hurt," Jet said, trying not to laugh.

Embarrassed, the turtle changed the subject. "I-I-I can do it. I just think we'd better not waste any more time."

"Okay, let's go," Missy said. She hoped that she could come back one day with MJ and play in the park. What fun they would have together!

"Hey, look. There's the picnic center. Maybe it will look familiar to Missy," Frankie said.

Chapter 6
Southern Hospitality

They stopped to look under one of the picnic tables in hopes of finding some leftover food. Out popped two ducks from under the next table. "Hi, y'all! What y'all doing?" one of the ducks said with a sweet southern accent.

The dog explained what they were doing there.

Missy asked the ducks, "What are your names? Where do you live?"

"Nice to meet you! My name is Breegirl, and this is my twin sister, Britt. We live here. Born and raised right here in the Lowcountry," Breegirl said proudly. "Our family lives in the pond too. Are y'all hungry?"

"Yes!" Missy said.

"Sure!" Jet said.

"Uh-huh!" Frankie said.

"Well, y'all have come to the right place." The ducks brought out a red-and-white-checkered tablecloth and spread out crackers, lettuce, and some leftover grits. They had a secret place in the woods where they hid all their goodies. They

loved to entertain guests.

The kitten tried the grits and said, "Wow, I've never had grits before. I guess...I kind of like them?"

Britt grinned at the cat's expression. "If you are southern, you will love grits."

"This is what you call southern hospitality!" Jet said. He was thankful for the food but secretly wished for a nice juicy bone.

Frankie was too busy eating the lettuce to talk. He nodded his head, happy for a bite to eat.

"Hey, y'all, there are probably some fresh fish scraps on the fishing dock. Want me to show you where?" Britt said.

Missy's head shot up. "Yes, please! Let's go! Hey, do you two want to go to live at my house? We have a nice pond."

"Oh, no thanks. We like it here. Our family is here. But we can visit you, and you can come see us anytime you want," Breegirl said.

"Okay, that would be very nice. Can you please show me the fishing dock?" Missy said.

Breegirl put her feathered wing to her chin. "My sister and I can still help you find your way home. If there is water by your house, we will find it. Besides, we are always up for a good adventure!"

Missy clasped her paws together. "Oh, thank you!" The kitten was so happy she had met such great new friends.

Chapter 7
Danger in the Park!

Off they trailed down Fisherman's Way to the fishing and crab pier. Sure enough, there were fish pieces at the end of the dock. Missy was just about to grab a piece when a flock of egrets dove in for the fish. "Hey, this is our territory."

The kitten backed away. "Sorry. I didn't know, Mr. Bird. I was just having a bite."

Jet bravely marched up to the egret. "Aw, come on, buddy. Let her have a little bite. You have the whole lake."

"Look, Mr. Dog, I have a family to feed," the egret said.

"That's okay, Jet. Let him feed his kids," Missy said, not wanting to cause any trouble.

The egret eyed the kitten and smiled. "You're okay, kitty. Go ahead and help yourself. I'll find some more fish." The beautiful bird and his family flew off, waving their wings.

"What a nice bird. Come on, guys. Let's dig in," Missy said.

"No thanks. Not for me. That's gross." The turtle closed his eyes and turned his head away.

"Okay, but you don't know what you're missing. Jet, do you want some?"

"I'll pass," the dog said.

Missy gulped down the fish and let out a big burp. She put her paw to her mouth, giggled, and said, "Excuuuse me."

"You're excused. Are you full now, Missy?" Jet asked.

"You betcha. I'm stuffed," Missy said.

They sat on the bench and watched the egrets, herons, cranes, and other birds fly by looking for a fish lunch. The green-and-yellow marsh grasses swayed back and forth in the breeze, making it look like the grass was waving at them. The tide was getting low, and Frankie pointed out the fid-dler crabs crawling around in the pluff mud. They decided it was time to go when a large copperhead snake slithered up out from under the rocks.

"Time to go, kids. He looks mean as a snake! Get it? Mean as a snake." Frankie laughed out loud. "Pretty funny, huh?" They all laughed and scattered down the pier to get away from the snake.

When they reached the platform of the dock, they thought they were safe, but out of the water appeared an alligator. Missy's eyes opened wide in terror. "OH MY! What is that?"

Jet grabbed Missy and said, "That is an alligator, and we need to get out of his way. We'll be snacks for him. MOVE IT!" They looked back to see the gator open his jaw wider to show them his sharp, jagged teeth. This made them run even faster to escape the alligator. Britt picked up the turtle and flew him out of harm's way.

Missy gasped. "He is not too friendly, is he?"

"Let's put it this way. You won't be asking the gator to come home with you," Breegirl said, grinning.

"What a day!" Frankie said.

"What an adventure!" Missy said.

They walked past signs for Marshview Circle and Osprey Point and on to the other side of the lake.

"Do you recognize the area, Missy?" Jet asked.

The kitten shook her head.

They passed the Splash Zone, a fun water spot where kids loved to play, and the climbing wall.

Missy looked at them with interest and asked, "Can we stop here? I would love to climb that wall. It looks like so much fun!"

"I think we should move on," Jet said. Then he noticed the disappointed look on Missy's face and added, "But we can come back another time and stay all day in the park if you want. Besides, don't you want to find your home?"

Missy nodded her head. "Yes, you're right, Jet! Let's go!"

Chapter 8
Pedal Faster!

As they walked past the campground, they came upon another large lake, which did not look familiar to Missy. "I'm getting tired and not getting any closer to finding my home."

"Don't be sad, my friend," Jet said. "Let's go across the lake, and if you don't recognize the area, we will go to the next park."

"I have a great idea, y'all," Britt said. "Since Missy is tired and Frankie is dragging his shell, let's take the pedal boats to the other side of the water. Breegirl and I have driven them many times before."

"Great idea, Britt!" Jet said.

Jet, Missy, and Frankie stepped into the back of one of the boats, while Breegirl and Britt sat in the front and pedaled. It was fun until they heard someone shout, "Who's in that boat? Come back here!"

"Pedal faster. Faster, you two!" Jet said to the ducks. "Let's get out of here before we get caught!" The ducks pedaled as fast as they could.

The sky grew dark when they reached the middle of the lake. A big shadow loomed over them. They looked up to see a huge eagle hovering above them.

The eagle swooped down in front of Missy. Jet immediately stepped in front of the kitten, growled, and swatted the eagle with his paw. "Get lost, you creep! Everybody, get down!"

Missy's heart pounded. Her body trembled in fear as she started to cry and hid behind Jet. The eagle soared up in the air, circling to plan his next attack.

Breegirl jumped up and said to her sister, "Take over for me, sis. I'm going to distract that bad bird." Breegirl flew off toward the eagle. Sure enough, the eagle chased the duck, allowing Britt to quickly maneuver the pedal boat to the other side of the lake. She hid the boat under some overgrown trees, and then they scrambled off into the woods until they were sure no one could spot them.

Breegirl caught up with them after she had lost the giant eagle. "Y'all okay?"

"We're okay. Are you all right? What happened?" Britt asked her sister.

"That crazy bird tried to eat me for lunch, but I was too fast for him." She picked off two loose feathers from her wing. "Darn it! How do I look with these missing feathers? Can you tell?" Bree-girl asked.

Britt hugged her. "You still look beautiful, sis. That was very brave and very stupid of you!"

Missy took a deep breath and said, "Thank you all for saving me!"

"Yeah, you guys. Nice work," the turtle said.

Britt and Breegirl did a high five and then a low five. Then they turned sideways and bumped their hips together. Then they twirled around to the opposite side and smacked hips again, praising each other. "Good job!" Britt said.

"Right on, sista!" Breegirl said.

Jet peeked around the bushes to see if anyone had followed them. "Too close for me! Look, little one. I think it's time to leave this park. We have looked pretty much everywhere. It's late afternoon, and I think we should go to the next park before it gets dark."

Chapter 9
A Storm Is Brewing!

Missy and Frankie hopped up on Jet's back so they could make better time and started down Fort Johnson Road to Demetre Park. The ducks flew directly overhead, like a protective umbrella. The wind picked up as they passed the deli, and it started to rain.

The kitten blinked the rain from her eyes. "Jet, this is where we met behind the deli. Maybe I live close by. You think?"

"Could be, Missy, but right now we need to hurry out of here. It's getting darker, and there's a storm brewing."

They reached Demetre Park, and the rain pounded down even harder. Jet could hardly see where he was going. "We'd better find shelter till the rain stops."

Missy shook off the rain as best she could and looked up at the darkened sky. The tree branches rocked back and forth like giant arms reaching for them. The murky shadows from the trees looked like dark, angry eyes staring at them.

The sights and the sounds of the woods frightened Missy.

A loud crack of thunder jolted Missy and made her jump. "I'm scared, Jet. The thunder is so loud." She put her paws over her ears.

Jet picked up the kitten and hugged her. "Don't be afraid. It's just a storm. Besides, thunder is just the angels bowling in heaven."

A grin spread across Missy's face. "Thank you, Jet.

I will never be spooked by that loud sound again."
She kissed his cheek. "I am so glad I found you!
I can't wait for you to meet MJ. You two are my
very best friends!"

Blushing, Jet carried Missy over by a tree to pro-
tect her from the wind.

Breegirl and Britt liked the rain but did not care
for the noisy wind tearing through the trees. They
all huddled under the tree for some protection.

Frankie caught up to them and said, "There's a big
hole in the tree over there. Maybe we can go inside till the storm stops."

"Good idea, Frankie," Jet said, "Let's go check it
out."

Chapter 10
No Room in the Tree

Wet and cold, Jet poked his head into the hole of the tree. He jumped back quickly when he heard, "This is my house!" Out sprang a chubby brown rabbit. "What do you want?" The bunny stared at the dog, the kitten, the turtle, and the two ducks, wondering if he should be worried.

"We mean no harm. We just wanted to get out of the storm," Jet said and explained to the rabbit what had happened to Missy.

"I am so sorry you lost your way, little kitty. I am very good with directions. Hold on a minute. I'll be right back." The rabbit went into the hole of the tree and came back out with a compass. "See? Now, which direction do you live? North, south, east, or west?"

The kitten felt like crying. "I don't know, Mr. Bunny."

"Don't you worry, little kitty. I'm a private investigator and will point you toward home when the storm is over."

"That would be great. What's your name?" Missy asked.

The bunny bowed at the waist. "Spunky Spankler—at your service, ma'am."

"Nice to meet you, Spunky."

Everyone shook the rabbit's paw. The wind whipped them around, almost knocking them over.

"We can't all stay in my tree. There is not enough room. But you do need to get out of this storm." Spunky thought for a moment and said, "There is a house close by where you could wait till the storm passes."

"Who lives in the house?" Jet asked.

"The Kellys live there in the summer. They go back to New York in the fall. They have two boys, Billy and Evan, whom I play with when they are here. Their big sister, Moey, feeds me. Come on. Let's hurry. The storm is getting worse."

When they reached the house, Jet asked, "How do we get in?"

"Easy. There's a mail slot on the front door. We could boost someone in, and they could slip into the slot and unlock the door." All eyes turned to the turtle, who was the smallest.

Jet was at the bottom of the stack. Next were Breegirl and Britt, and then Spunky and Missy. Frankie was at the top of the heap. The turtle slipped through the mail slot and fell onto the floor inside the house with a big thud. "Ouch!" Frankie shouted.

"Hurry up and open the door!" Thunder boomed and a lightning strike in the distance lit up the sky like a scary movie.

"Frankie, are you all right?" Missy asked.

"Yes, I'm okay," the turtle replied.

"Snap it up, and open the door," Jet said.

"Patience, my friends. Have you ever known a fast turtle?"

The group laughed. "You have a point there, buddy," Jet said.

Once inside, Spunky found the linen closet and gave everyone a big, fluffy towel to dry off. Then he gave Jet his compass and excused himself.

"I need to get back to the park. My wife is about to deliver our first babies. It looks like triplets!" the proud papa said. Everyone congratulated and thanked the bunny.

Spunky turned, waved good-bye, and said, "Y'all come back and visit us. The missus and I would love you all over for some carrot stew."

Chapter 11
"Tough Guy" Munchie

They went into the kitchen in search of some food and found crackers, vegetables, and some sardines. While they were nibbling on their treats, a mouse appeared and yelled, "Hey, that's my food!" The mouse was very scary looking, with big front teeth; one was cracked in half. The mouse also had a large scar under one eye.

Everyone backed up. "Sorry we bothered you. We just wanted to dry off and get out of the storm. We will leave," Missy said.

The mouse glared at them. "This is my house when everyone is gone. And when they are here in the summer, I hide and come out at night and trick their dopey cat, Bruno."

The kitten quickly hid behind Jet. She did not like the angry look in the mouse's eyes when he talked about Bruno.

"I won't hurt you if you just leave me alone. The last cat I tangled with did this to me." The mouse touched the scar under his eye.

"Hey, man, we're not here to hurt anyone. We'll leave," Jet said.

"Wait a minute," the mouse said. "You can stay till morning. Just stay out of my way."

"Thank you so much!" Missy said. "What is your name?"

"I'm Munchie," he grumbled. "Just leave in the morning." The mouse disappeared into a chewed hole in the corner.

"Wow, he's grouchy and mean. I don't like him," Frankie said. "His name should be Monster or Meanie, not Munchie."

"I think he's all right," Missy said. "He's scared, and I bet he has no family to care for him. Maybe we can talk him into coming with us to find my home."

Chapter 12
The Wise Ole Owl

All of a sudden, a gust of chilly wind blew the door open and whistled through the room. A drenched owl stood at the doorway.

"Who are you?" Jet asked.

The owl shivered from the cold. "I'm Oliver. May I please come in? I saw you enter the house from that tree over there."

"Hurry in, and close the door," Jet said.

The owl entered the room. "Whooo...it's bad out there. It's even too windy for a bird. What are you all doing here?"

Jet told the owl the tale of Missy getting lost and how they were helping her find her way home.

"I have excellent eyesight, especially at night. I'd like to help," Oliver said.

"That would be great. Do you have a family?" Missy asked.

"No. I wish I did," Oliver replied as he shook his wings.

"I could share my family with you, Oliver," Missy said.

"That would be quite super! Thank you!" the owl said.

Chapter 13
Get Your Hats On! It's Party Time!

"Hey, y'all, come and see what we found."

They turned around to see Breegirl and Britt prance out of the bedroom wearing big red hats, jewelry, and brightly colored scarves. They even had colorful little red-and-purple purses draped over their arms. "There's really cool stuff in the closet. Come on, y'all. Put a hat on, and we'll have a party."

"Okay!" Missy said. "What fun we'll have!"

Jet, Frankie, and Oliver looked at each other, "Girls!" Jet said. "They are so weird sometimes!"

Frankie agreed with Jet. "They sure are!"

Being the wise ole owl, Oliver said, "I think it's a cute idea. Let them have their fun."

Missy wanted everyone to be happy. "Come on, guys. Join us, and pick out a hat. There's boy's stuff in here too."

Jet and Frankie sighed and then gave in and went to the closet to pick out their hats. The turtle chose a sailor hat. The dog selected a cowboy hat and grabbed a guitar from the closet. Oliver put on a captain's hat and felt proud as he looked into the mirror.

The large red hats swallowed Missy up, making her disappear. Britt fixed her up by tying a red scarf around her head like a headband. Then she stuck a purple feather in it. Missy found a strand of pearls and hung them around her neck. She grabbed a pair of red high-heeled shoes that were way too big and made her waddle.

"Hey, Missy, you waddle like us now. You could be a duck," Britt said.

"Ya think?" Breegirl looked at her sister and they both quacked up laughing.

"What's with the red hats?" Oliver asked.

"I read about this Red Hat Club in the paper," Jet said. "It's a group of ladies that get together once a month for lunch or some social gathering."

"Sounds stupid to me," Frankie said, feeling foolish in his hat.

"It's not stupid! They have a great time!" Breegirl flapped her wing at him.

"GIRLS!" Jet and Frankie said in unison.

"I think it's cool!" Missy smiled. "I'll tell you what. When we get home, let's start our own Red Hat Group!"

"That would be awesome, Missy!" the ducks shouted out, flapping their wings.

"We'll call ourselves the Red Hat Kit Kats!" Missy said.

"How about the Red Hat Daffy Ducks?" Britt shouted.

Missy put on the stereo and blasted, "WHO LET THE DOGS OUT! WOOF...WOOF...WOOF... WOOF!"

Jet let out a bark of laughter. "Very funny!" He had to admit he enjoyed the music and the playful mood of the girls.

"What are you fools doing?"

Everyone stopped to see Munchie the mouse. He had his arms crossed and was frowning at them.

"We are having a party. Want to join in?" Missy asked.

"No way! And keep that music down! Do you want to attract attention with all that racket?"

"No one will hear the music, dude. There's a storm going on," Jet said. It was true. The storm had gotten worse.

"You'd better put everything back where you found it, or I'll get blamed for the mess," Munchie squeaked in anger. He felt he had to keep up his tough-guy image so no one would mess with him. What he really wanted to do was join the party. It had been a long time since he'd had friends or family.

Missy sensed that he really wanted to stay and share in the good times. Maybe he was not the tough guy he pretended to be. She had a feeling that his squeak was worse than his bite. Giggling, Missy thought, "I am getting funny now, just like Jet and Frankie."

"Oh, come on, Munchie. The boys need you here. I have just the hat for you!"

"Forget about it! It's not going to happen!" the mouse said with disgust.

Missy knew he would not go for a frilly hat, so she picked out a Brooklyn Dodgers baseball cap. "Here, try this one out, you look like a baseball fan to me."

A tiny smile appeared on Munchie's face. "I love baseball! I went to Brooklyn Dodgers games with my father years ago in New York, before they moved to LA. I never missed a game. There's nothing better than watching baseball with a big ole meatball-and-cheese sub and a cold one!"

"Bingo! We got him!"

Missy put another CD on.

TAKE ME OUT TO THE BALLGAME
TAKE ME OUT WITH THE CROWD
BUY ME SOME PEANUTS AND CRACKERJACKS
I DON'T CARE IF I EVER GET BACK
FOR IT'S ROOT, ROOT, ROOT FOR THE HOME TEAM

IF THEY DON'T WIN, IT'S A SHAME
FOR ITS ONE, TWO, THREE STRIKES YOU'RE
OUT
AT THE OLD BALLGAME

Munchie sang along with the music, not too well, but no one minded because he was having fun.

Then the mouse even went into the kitchen and came back out with peanuts and popcorn that he had stashed away.

The party continued till 3:00 a.m., when they finally turned off the music and stretched out on the floor. They all felt like old friends and vowed to start out in the morning to find Missy's home.

Munchie whispered to Missy before going off to sleep, "Thank you for inviting me to the party. I had a great time. Can I go with you in the morning to help you find your family? Not that I mind staying here alone. It's just that I think you need someone tough to help you find your way."

Missy smiled at her new "tough" friend, "That's a good idea. I could use your help. Good night, Munchie."

"Good night, Missy. Sleep tight. Don't let the bedbugs bite," Munchie said.

The kitten dropped right off to dreamland, as did

Breegirl and Britt. Munchie was too excited to sleep. He saw the light on in the kitchen and noticed that Jet, Frankie, and Oliver were not in the living room. He tiptoed from the room to see what the boys were up to.

Chapter 14
Read, Dream, and Write!

The dog, the turtle, and the owl were sitting around the kitchen counter. They stopped their conversation when the mouse entered. "I hope we didn't wake you," Jet said.

"No, man. I couldn't sleep. Can I join you guys?" Munchie said.

"Sure you can. Climb up on a chair," Jet said.

"What are talking about?" Munchie asked.

"Oliver was just telling us he wants to write a book. He loves to read and has a stack of books in his tree house."

"Really? I've never read a book," Munchie said and quickly added, "but I can read. I've read sports magazines."

Oliver looked at the mouse over his glasses, "Buddy, you've got to start reading books. It takes you to places you never imagined. I have just the book for you to read. It's called *The Mouse and the Motorcycle,* by Beverly Cleary. I think you will enjoy that book. In fact, there are many books about mice and their adventures. I will give them to you in the morning."

"Thanks. Does the mouse really have a motorcycle?" Munchie asked.

"Yes. Anything can happen in a book. Would you like to ride a motorcycle?"

The mouse thought for a moment, resting his head on his hand. "No. I'd rather have a race car or a convertible." He closed his eyes and said, "I can imagine myself driving down the highway, with the top down, wind blowing in my fur, sunglasses on, and the radio blasting the sound track of *The Lion King*. I could stand up to a lion! Sure I could! As a matter of fact, I could be a lion!" Jet, Oliver, and Frankie had to look away to hide their smiles.

"Yeah, right!" Frankie whispered to Jet.

Oliver was pleased that the mouse was interested in reading. "You can stretch your imagination and have any kind of adventure you want from books."

Munchie's mind wandered on. "Maybe I could even get a girlfriend to ride with me."

"Where would you go if you had a car?" Jet asked.

"Well, maybe drive down to baseball spring training in Florida and catch the Braves, Indians, Yankees, Mets, and Marlins play. Then I would drive up to New York and see some of my buddies in Brooklyn. They have the best deli food. I would grab some crusty Italian bread and a big chunk of cheese...ah, I can smell the aroma now! Next I would go to this Italian bakery I used to go to and get some warm cookies. Come to think of it, I knew this sweet mouse, Jade, who used to work at the bakery. Maybe she would like to take a ride with me."

"See, books make you dream and imagine all kinds of things," the owl said.

"What do you want to write about, Oliver?" Munchie asked.

"An adventure story, but I am stuck on a plot," Oliver said.

Jet grinned and slapped Oliver on the back. "Well,

my friend, grab your pencil and paper. I have just the tale of adventure you're searching for."

For the next hour, Jet told the story of Missy's lost adventure, while Oliver wrote down every detail on his pad.

"This is good stuff. Tell me more." Oliver was so excited to finally write his book. He could see himself signing books at Barnes and Noble, Books-A-Million, the local libraries, schools, and so forth. He would also hand out his books to all his friends in the woods.

By the time they finished, the sun had peeked through the window, and the birds outside had begun their early morning songs. They decided to grab a few hours of sleep before the girls woke up. Frankie and Munchie were asleep on their chair, both snoring loudly.

Chapter 15
Breakfast

The group woke up to the smell and sounds of sizzling bacon coming from the kitchen.

"Wow, does that smell good!" Jet said, licking his chops.

"I'll second that!" Frankie said as he poked his head out from his shell. "Who's cooking?"

"I am. Wake up, sleepyheads," Munchie said, as he came out of the kitchen wearing an apron that read KISS THE CHEF. "Come and eat while it's hot. We have a big day ahead. We need to get Missy home!"

They all marched into the kitchen cautiously. They were not too sure about Munchie's good mood, even though he had been nicer at the party. They thought, "Why is he being so nice?"

Missy knew that the tough-guy act was a cover. He was really a good guy inside.

They enjoyed a great breakfast of scrambled eggs, bacon, sausage, toast, and milk. Everyone praised the mouse for his cooking skills and thanked him over and over. They were starting to think that Missy was right: the mouse was an okay fellow after all.

Munchie blushed from all the compliments. "Okay, guys. Now that we have full bellies, we need to clean up the house and head out."

"Yes, yes, let's get going! I am so excited! Munchie is going to help us. He is not sure about living with my family yet."

After vacuuming, washing the dishes, and returning their party hats back to the closet, they set out to the park across the road.

Chapter 16
Demetre Park

They walked into Demetre Park with high hopes that it would look familiar to Missy. They were immediately hit by the beautiful view of the Charleston Harbor. Directly in front of them was an incredible bridge, stretching across the harbor.

"That is a beautiful bridge," Missy said.

"That's the new Ravenel Bridge," Oliver said proudly.

"Awesome!" the group said.

"Yes, it is." The owl looked at the bridge and was amazed at what he saw. In his mind he saw big silver strings reaching for giant stone columns that stretched across the water. He took his sketchpad out and drew it for his book.

To the left was the James Island Yacht Club. Munchie boasted that he had snuck on one of the boats and taken a ride one night.

"Lucky you. I'd love to cruise on a boat sometime," Jet said. 'I'm too big to sneak on, though."

"That's one advantage to being small. I can hide. Maybe next summer I could sneak you on board," Munchie said.

"That would be neat," Jet said.

"I want to go too," the turtle said, wanting to be included with the boys.

"I'll see what I can arrange," the mouse said.

They walked along the sandy beach, where the turtle inched toward a horseshoe crab, unable to capture it.

"I could catch that crab!" Munchie boasted.

"Come on, y'all. We are not here to play. We need to help Missy," Britt said.

The boys agreed to get back to the task and find clues that would lead to the kitten's home.

"Britt is right. Does anything look familiar to you, Missy?" Jet asked.

The kitten turned around in circles, looking around the park. Crying, she said, "I don't know. I'm never going to find my home." She put her head in her paws and sobbed. "I want to go home! I miss MJ!"

Jet put his paws around her, lifted her up, and wiped the tears from her eyes. The owl offered her a handkerchief. She blew her nose loudly, like a horn. The ducks both had tears in their eyes. Even tough-guy Munchie had to turn away from the group, saying he had something in his eye.

"Don't cry, little one. We'll think of something," Jet said.

"Yeah, we won't stop till we find your home. We promise!" Frankie said.

"Thanks, guys," Missy said between sobs.

Chapter 17
Finding Home!

"I know where you live, kitty."

Missy glanced up and rubbed her eyes to see the bright-blue flying creature that she had chased to the park.

"It's you!" Missy cried out. "You're the reason I'm lost!"

Missy's friends all stared at the bluebird, giving her the evil eye.

"Whoa, hold on there. I did not make her follow me. It's not my fault!" The bluebird backed away from the group.

The kitten realized the fluttering creature was right. "I'm sorry I yelled at you. I'm just so sad. I cannot find my way home, and my friends here are trying to help me." She introduced everyone. "Who are you? What is your name?"

"I am a bluebird, and my name is Beth. Nice to meet you."

"Did you say you know where Missy lives?" Jet asked.

"Sure I do! She lives right down the road on Sweet-pea Road. I love that house. They have beautiful flowers all over the yard. Do you want me to take you there?"

Munchie rolled his eyes up and said, "Like, yeah, Miss Bluebird. That's the purpose of our journey."

Missy leapt up and down with excitement. "Yahoo! We're going home!" Jet wagged his tail high and fast.

The group clapped, cheered, and laughed, happy that the little kitten was going home.

Chapter 18
Family Reunion!

It looked like a parade going down the road. Beth was up in the air, leading the way. She was followed by Missy, Jet, Oliver, Breegirl, Britt, and Munchie. Last trailed Frankie, trying to keep up.

They rounded the corner to Sweetpea Road, and Missy smiled and shouted, "It's my street! I see my house!" The kitten started skipping and broke into a sprint when she saw her house.

Just then, her front door opened, and MJ stepped out onto the front steps, where she had kept watch for her kitten all day. MJ heard a loud meow. She turned and spotted her beloved kitty cat running down the road.

MJ ran toward the kitten, screaming, "MISSY! MISSY! I have been so worried about you!" MJ scooped her kitten in her arms, laughing and crying with happiness.

Missy hugged and licked MJ's face with kisses. "I was lost and couldn't find my way back home. My friends here helped me. I'm so glad to be home!" Missy buried her face in the little girl's neck, purring with happiness.

"Don't you ever roam off again! I thought I'd lost you forever." MJ knew she should be angry at the kitten for running away, but she was too grateful to have her back home.

"Who are your friends?" MJ asked.

Missy introduced her buddies to MJ, and she thanked them for helping her kitten find her way home.

"Wait a minute. Where's Frankie?" Missy looked around in panic, "Oh no, is he lost now?" Everyone rushed out to the street and started laughing. Frankie was still lumbering along the road.

Jet hurried to the turtle and hoisted him up on his back. He dropped Frankie off in front of Missy. The kitten was relieved to see her friend. Missy explained to MJ that some of her friends had no homes. She wondered if the family could adopt them, like they did her.

MJ smiled and said, "Well, let's go ask my parents."

The Richards were thrilled that Missy was safe. When asked if they could adopt some of Missy's friends, Mrs. Richard said, "Who wants to be adopted?"

Missy said, "Well, this is Jet. He's not sure if he wants to stay. His family was mean to him, so he ran away."

Jet lowered his head and became shy, not sure what he wanted to do.

Mrs. Richard smiled at the dog. "I'm sorry your family was mean to you, Jet. How about you give us a trial run to see if you want to stay?"

"Please, please say yes, Jet! You are my best buddy!" Missy pleaded.

"All right, Missy. I'll give it a try, just for you," Jet said.

"YAY!" Missy cheered and clapped her paws together.

"You can stay in the house, Jet. There will be rules, but we will take good care of you and give you a loving home."

"Thank you!" Jet said.

Breegirl and Britt headed out to fly to Goose Creek to visit some family. They would then return home to James Island County Park, but they promised to stay in touch and visit often. "Don't forget we have to think about our Red Hat Club," Britt said.

"I won't forget, and thanks again! We will visit soon," Missy said, waving good-bye as the ducks flew off.

Frankie was thrilled to live in the pond in the backyard. He was excited to have a home and a family.

In addition, the turtle would have a new pond to explore.

Mrs. Richard looked at the mouse, having doubts about keeping him, "What are you going to do, Munchie? If you decide to stay, you can live in the garage, but only if you promise to behave yourself and not chew it up."

Munchie thought for a moment and surprised everyone by saying, "I would like to stay with you when the Kellys are gone, if that's okay. Not that I mind staying alone or that I'm lonely. I think I can help Jet look after Missy. In addition, I have a lot of reading to catch up on." He winked at the owl. "And another thing," the mouse said, grinning, "I kind of like bugging and driving that fat cat, Bruno, nuts. I have some new tricks to try out on him. For the most part, I enjoy playing cat-and-mouse games with him as long has he doesn't get too rough." Munchie touched his scar. "Bruno is getting older now and not moving too fast, so I can outrun him. Besides, the fat cat might get bored and fatter yet if I'm not there to make him chase me."

Missy was happy that her tough-guy friend Munchie had decided to stay with her on a part-time basis.

The bluebird Beth said that she would visit Missy when she played in her yard and wave to her through the window. Beth promised she would not make Missy chase her again.

"That leaves you, Oliver. We have many trees in the backyard, and we have a tree house. We could put some shelves up to store all your books. There is a desk and chair in the tree house too, since I hear you are writing a book," Mrs. Richard said.

The owl was speechless and just nodded in agreement. Oliver was amazed at his luck and thought how great his new home would be.

Chapter 19
Family and Friends!

Everyone was happy, especially Missy. She had her family again and along the way had found new best friends. Life was good.

The kitten was not about to wander off anytime soon, especially without Jet or MJ. She had maps of the area to study before she would ever attempt a venture off the property again. She planned to visit Breegirl and Britt and check out Spunky's new family. Missy and Jet even planned a trip back to James Island County Park. This time, MJ would go with them. Munchie wanted to go too, for protection, of course, but it was getting harder and harder to get him out of the house. He was too busy reading. Oliver happily kept him well stocked with adventure books from his book stash and from the Charleston County Library. Munchie even had his own library card now.

Oliver had an idea for his next book. It would be about a mouse from Brooklyn who wanted to be a lion. The owl chuckled just thinking about it and knew Munchie would love that one.

After a couple of weeks, Jet decided he was ready to be adopted. He finally had the family he'd always wanted. It was so nice to trust again and to be with people who cared about him. Jet had learned he did not have to be afraid of people after all. Missy and Jet were like two peas in a pod, always together. They took naps together on their favorite blanket by the window and soaked up the sun. When MJ came home from school, the three of them played in the yard till dinner. Jet protected Missy and MJ, and in return Missy and MJ fussed over him, telling him often how much they loved him. Missy considered Jet her big, brave, smart brother now.

Chapter 20
Three Months Later...
Oliver's Book

Oliver wrote every night for three months before he was satisfied that his book was ready to send out. The only problem was the title. He could not seem to come up with anything that knocked his socks off. He had suggestions from all his friends, but he still couldn't come up with a proper name for his masterpiece.

Missy finally hit a home run for the title when she watched Lowcountry Live on TV with Jet one morning.

Missy and the dog loved to watch Lowcountry Live, learning all about Charleston. They even had animals on the show. Missy loved the cooking segments, which always made her hungry.

Watching Lowcountry Live one Tuesday morning, Missy jumped up from the couch and yelled, "I've got it! Come on, Jet. Let's go out to the tree house! I need to see Oliver right away!"

They ran out of the house and up the ladder. They knocked on the door and then pushed their way into the tree house. "Oliver, wake up! Wake up!" They shook the owl until he opened one eyelid.

"Whooo? What? What's going on?" The owl yawned.

"Open your eyes. I've got a great title for your book!"

Oliver's other eyelid popped open. "What is it?"

"What do think of A Lowcountry Adventure?" Missy asked.

Oliver grinned. He liked it. He thought for a moment and said, "I'll do you one better. How about *Missy's Lowcountry Adventure*? Awesome! Let me get my glasses on and get my pen!"

Missy turned toward Jet for his approval. "What do you think, Jet?"

Jet gave Missy a big smile and a thumbs-up sign. "Perfect! I love it!"

Missy beamed with delight. She loved it too!

The End

Word Search for characters in Missy's Lowcountry Adventure

```
N B Z M T M D H I Y B B I L L
C B D U C K S Z E M C U R Q C
F R A N K I E Z B M K N J W O
C E J C U T I L L Z Y N A N M
B E T H A T S P U N K Y D O G
M G F I J E T O E A G L E R M
W I P E P N U Y B R T M T N F
Y R O W L M R M I S S Y R K K
A L L I G A T O R F M U B V F
B R I T T A L U D V U O V J T
K E V A N A E S H I Q W H H S
M O E Y V C F E A C T T M E A
J B R A B Y F D T B R P K M B
L V L D U S K M Q O R Q T K M
H Q M I Q Q G X T C Z N T J B
```

Alligator	Beth	Bill	Bluebird	Breegirl
Britt	Bunny	Dog	Ducks	Eagle
Evan	Frankie	Jade	Jet	Kitten
Missy	MJ	Moey	Mouse	Munchie
Oliver	Owl	Spunky	Turtle	

Trivia & Fun Facts
Did you know...?

Cats:

- A cat has 230 bones in its body.

- Cats make about 100 different sounds, dogs make about 10.

- Female cats tend to right-pawed, male cats are usually left-pawed.

- A cat has no collarbone, so he can fit through any opening the size of their heads.

- A cats nose has ridges, just like a human's fingerprint.

- The average cat sleeps around 13-18 hours a day.

Dogs:

- Dogs have sweat glands in-between their paws.

- Dog nose prints are as unique as human fingerprints and be used to ID them.

- The average dog can run about 19 miles per hour.

- Greyhounds are the fastest dogs and can run at the speed of 45 miles per hour.

- Dogs see much better than humans at night because they have a special light reflecting layer behind their eyes.

- Dogs cannot eat raisins, grapes,onions or chocolate because it makes them sick.

Bluebirds:

- Bluebirds can be attracted to peanut butter mixes and fruit. The bluebird's favorite is mealworms.

- If a birdbath is available, the Eastern bluebird will find it. If water is moving, so much the better.

- The Eastern bluebird is an extremely social creature. They gather in large flocks of 100 or more.

Owls:

- The neck of an owl is so flexible that it can rotate its head $\frac{3}{4}$ of the way around.

- Owls do not make nests.

- An owl has 3 eyelids; 1 for blinking, 1 for sleeping and 1 for keeping the eye clean and healthy.

Rabbits:

- Rabbits can purr similar to a cat.

- Rabbits do not hibernate.

- When rabbits are happy, they jump and twist, this is called a binky.

- Rabbits can see behind them without turning their heads, but they do have a blind spot in front of their face.

- Rabbits can learn their names and simple words such as "No."

Ducks:

- A girl duck or hen makes a loud QUACK sound, while a boy duck or drake has a raspy, muffled call.

- Ducks sleep with half their brains awake. Ducks are more likely to sleep with one eye open when they are located on the edge of sleeping groups. They can detect predators in less than a second.

- Ducks can live 20 or more years with good care and feeding. The world's record is held by a Mallard Drake that lived 27 years...Quacktastic!

- Ducks have very good vision, they can see in color.

Turtles:

- Turtles cannot stick out their tongues.

- On flat ground, a North American soft shell turtle can outrun a human!

- Sea turtles can swim up to 35 miles per hour.

- Many people still believe that turtles can come out of their shells...guess what? They can't!

- Many turtles are expert climbers.

Mice:

- On average, a mouse's tail is as long as it's body.

- A mouse has 16 teeth and 18 toes.

- The average mouse will breathe 163 times a minute.

- Mice can travel while hanging upside down.

Eagles:

- Bald eagles are not really bald. They have white feathers on their heads.

- The wingspan of an eagle measures from 5.5 to 7.5 feet.

- Did you know that bald eagles have re-markably good eyesight? They can see 4 to 7 times better than people can. They can see things from a far distance of up to 1 mile.

- When a bald eagle migrates south it al-ways goes to the same spot and when it returns north it always goes to the same spot.

- An Eagle's nest can range in size from 5 feet in diameter to the exceptional 9 feet in diameter.

Alligators:

- Alligators date back 200 million years.

- The largest alligator ever recorded in the Everglades National Park in Florida was 17 feet 5 inches.

- Alligators are generally shy and try to avoid humans.

- More than 1/2 the alligators sited in South Carolina are less than 5 feet long and weigh about 22 pounds. Alligators this size feed on crawfish, small snakes, frogs and turtles...WATCH OUT FRANKIE!

- An adult alligator can become quite large at about 13 feet long.

Author:

Marilyn (Esper) Kelsey is from Vermilion, Ohio. Lived in beautiful Charleston, South Carolina, the setting of Missy's Lowcountry Adventure, for seventeen years. She currently lives in Millsboro, Delaware, to be closer to her children and grandchildren.

A registered nurse for forty-five years, she is married with three children and three granddaughters.

Marilyn has been a member of several different writers organizations, including a Charleston writer's group, South Carolina Writers and Illustrators, Rehoboth Writer's Guild, and The Mystery Writers of America.

Illustrator:

Karri Stafford lives in Delaware. She always loved to draw and carried her sketchbook around to draw whenever time allowed, between working and being a busy mother of five children (three girls and two boys).

Marilyn met Karri in the Hair Salon where Karri was employed and noticed her drawing on her sketchpad and the illustrations were created!

Made in the USA
San Bernardino, CA
26 October 2016